Stan the Dog and the Sneaky Snacks

written and illustrated by
Scoular Anderson

PICTURE WINDOW BOOKS
Minneapolis, Minnesota

For Ailsa

Editor: Jill Kalz
Page Production: Brandie E. Shoemaker
Creative Director: Keith Griffin
Editorial Director: Carol Jones

First American edition published in 2007 by
Picture Window Books
5115 Excelsior Boulevard
Suite 232
Minneapolis, MN 55416
877-845-8392
www.picturewindowbooks.com

First published in 2002 by A&C Black Publishers Limited, 38 Soho Square,
London W1D 3HB, with the title STAN AND THE SNEAKY SNACKS
Text and illustrations copyright © Scoular Anderson 2002

Printed in the United States of America.

Library of Congress Cataloging-in-Publication Data
Anderson, Scoular.
Stan the dog and the sneaky snacks / by Scoular Anderson. -- 1st American ed.
p. cm. — (Read-it! chapter books)
Summary: Stan the dog has to go along when his owner takes up jogging so
the clever canine spends his exercise time planning to get back to his favorite
pastimes of eating and sleeping.
ISBN-13: 978-1-4048-2742-4 (hardcover)
ISBN-10: 1-4048-2742-0 (hardcover)
[1. Dogs—Fiction. 2. Running—Fiction. 3. Snack foods—Fiction.] I. Title.
II. Series.
PZ7.A5495Sts 2006
[E]—dc22   2006005754

Table of Contents

Chapter One

It was the weekend, so Stan was happy. Everyone was home. Big Belly and Can Opener didn't go to work on weekends. Crumble and Handout didn't go to school either. More people around the house meant more food for Stan.

Stan waited for everyone to get up.

Big Belly was the first one downstairs.

He opened the back door to let
Stan out.

OK, Stan.
Hurry up!

STRETCH

STRETCH

Stan wandered through the yard.

He did what he
was supposed
to do.

Then he went to the back gate and
looked into the alley.

The schoolkids took a shortcut through the alley, so there were always bits of food lying around.

Big Belly had put a latch high on the gate to keep Stan from getting out into the alley.

Stan checked that no one was looking.

He reached up ...

... clicked the latch ...

CLICK!

... and went out into the alley.

Stan ate the
half-hamburger.

He found a bag
of chips with
several chips
still in it.

He found a
green gumdrop.

Then he found some melted ice cream.

After his alley snack, Stan wandered back into the yard and pushed the gate shut.

He stopped at the bird feeder.

He pushed open the back door and walked into the kitchen.

Chapter Two

Big Belly had cooked himself some bacon for breakfast. Crumble and Handout were already at the table eating cereal and toast. Stan went to his usual place under the table.

Crumble was dropping crumbs everywhere. There were already quite a few for Stan to lick up.

Stan knew he'd get a snack from Handout, so he sat very close.

Suddenly, there was a horrible shriek.

Can Opener had walked in.

In a flash, Stan ran out from under
the table and stood beside his bowl.

But the bacon went into the trash.

Stan went back under the table.

Breakfast continued.

After breakfast, Stan went to doze in his bed. He was having a wonderful dream, when ...

... a noise woke him up.

But Stan was wrong.

Big Belly was standing in the hall,
holding Stan's leash.

Stan was horrified.

Big Belly took Stan out the back door. The rest of the family came to see them off.

Big Belly jogged across the yard, out the back gate, and into the alley.

Chapter Three

Jogging with Big Belly wasn't much fun. His big feet went FLIP, FLAP, FLIP, FLAP on the ground.

His belly went WOBBLE, WOBBLE.

His bottom went WIBBLE, WIBBLE.

By the time they got to the end of the alley, Big Belly was already out of breath and red in the face.

Big Belly dug in one of the pockets
of his shorts and brought out a big
bar of ...

He dug in the other pocket.

Just then, Big Belly dropped them,
and Stan leapt forward.

He'd keep Big Belly out of trouble!

But Big Belly was not pleased.

Big Belly started jogging again. It was more of a walk than a jog. He and Stan went down the street and turned left at the traffic lights.

It was the way to Dino's café.

Big Belly tied Stan's leash to a table.

He went into the café.

After a few minutes, Stan was bored. A woman passed, eating a bag of potato chips.

She threw the bag into a trash can.

The bag teetered on the edge.

Then it fell out.

Stan stretched to reach the chips ...

... but a sudden gust of wind blew
the bag away.

Stan really wanted that bag.

Big Belly was just finishing his bacon
and eggs, when he saw something
out of the corner of his eye. It was
the table umbrella.

The umbrella moved one way and
then back the other way.

Then it toppled over and caught one of the hanging baskets as it fell.

There was a thump, a bang, and then a shriek. Big Belly leapt up from his table and ran outside.

Big Belly got Stan untangled, and
then they walked quickly home
through the park.

The rest of the family was waiting for them.

Chapter Four

Stan was lying in his basket, having another wonderful dream.

It was Sunday morning. The family wouldn't be up for a long, long time.

Then Stan heard two noises he didn't like. The first noise came from the bathroom. Someone was awake.

GURGLE... ...GURRRGLE...

He thought he had better check out the second noise. He walked down the hall and into the living room. He climbed up onto a chair by the window and looked out.

Rain! I thought so. I'm not going out in that!

On the way back to the kitchen, Stan got a shock. There was Big Belly.

They went out the back door and headed to the park.

Stan was miserable. Big Belly's feet splashed in all of the puddles.

Jogging wasn't fun at all. There was no time to stop and sniff interesting things, like lampposts and trash cans.

Just as they were about to reach the pond, Stan spotted something.

Oh, no! It's Pongo and Fangs! I can't let them see me like this!

Stan stopped.

The leash slipped out of Big Belly's hand, and he flew forward.

He skidded in a puddle and dove over a park bench.

Big Belly was not pleased.

Stan turned and ran.

He dodged past Pongo and Fangs.

He didn't stop running until he was safely back home.

Chapter Five

When Big Belly got home, he was exhausted. He had chased Stan all the way. Can Opener took care of all of his bumps and bruises.

Can Opener wasn't going to let Big
Belly rest too long.

Soon lunch came—Stan's favorite moment of the day. Can Opener opened a can of Dogzo for Stan.

After that, the family was busy. Big Belly washed the car.

Can Opener tidied the yard.

Crumble and Handout played soccer.

Normally, Stan liked to play soccer, too, but he was worried about another jog. He wasn't comfy in his bed.

He wasn't comfy on the sofa.

Sigh.

He wandered from room to room.

Just then, he saw a red light blinking on the telephone.

Stan pressed a button ...

... and then listened to the message.

Stan found this message very interesting.

Later in the afternoon, Can Opener got in the car and drove away.

Big Belly was reading the Sunday papers.

Crumble and Handout were playing a computer game.

Stan knew it was time for his walk.
He stared at Big Belly and whined.

Eventually, Stan had to take drastic
action. He pounced.

Big Belly wasn't in a good mood.
And the children had been dragged
away from their game, so they
weren't in a good mood either.

Stan kept dragging them the opposite
way from the park.

Stan pulled Crumble, Handout, and
Big Belly all the way to Dino's.

They all pressed their noses against
the window.

Can Opener and Big Belly had some explaining to do.

Once they got back home, the family set off again, jogging to the park. Stan was happy to let them go.

Look for More
Read-it!
Chapter Books

Grandpa's Boneshaker Bicycle	978-1-4048-2732-5
Jenny the Joker	978-1-4048-2733-2
Little T and Lizard the Wizard	978-1-4048-2725-7
Little T and the Crown Jewels	978-1-4048-2726-4
Little T and the Dragon's Tooth	978-1-4048-2727-1
Little T and the Royal Roar	978-1-4048-2728-8
The Minestrone Mob	978-1-4048-2723-3
Mr. Croc Forgot	978-1-4048-2731-8
Mr. Croc's Silly Sock	978-1-4048-2730-1
Mr. Croc's Walk	978-1-4048-2729-5
The Peanut Prankster	978-1-4048-2724-0
Silly Sausage and the Little Visitor	978-1-4048-2735-6
Silly Sausage and the Spooks	978-1-4048-2736-3
Silly Sausage Goes to School	978-1-4048-2738-7
Silly Sausage in Trouble	978-1-4048-2737-0
Stan the Dog and the Crafty Cats	978-1-4048-2739-4
Stan the Dog and the Golden Goals	978-1-4048-2740-0
Stan the Dog and the Major Makeover	978-1-4048-2741-7
Uncle Pat and Auntie Pat	978-1-4048-2734-9

Looking for a specific title? A complete list
of *Read-it!* Chapter Books is available on our Web site:
www.picturewindowbooks.com

OCT 0 8